# Sigmund B...

# Watch Out for Joel!

## Bad Bug Blues

**BETHANY BACKYARD®**
www.bethanyhouse.com

*Bad Bug Blues*
Copyright © 2002
Sigmund Brouwer

Cover and interior illustrations by Tammie Lyon
Cover design by Jennifer Parker

Published by Bethany House Publishers
11400 Hampshire Avenue South
Bloomington, Minnesota 55438
www.bethanyhouse.com

Bethany House Publishers is a Division of
Baker Book House Company, Grand Rapids, Michigan.

Printed in China

**Library of Congress Cataloging-in-Publication Data**

Brouwer, Sigmund, 1959–
   Bad bug blues / by Sigmund Brouwer.
     p. cm. — (Watch out for Joel!)
Summary: Ricky and Joel are treated to a concert by their neighbor, Mr. Jones.
   ISBN 0-7642-2580-4
   [1. Concerts—Fiction.] I. Title.
PZ7.B79984 Bad   2002
[Fic]—dc21

                                    2002006130

# Be Kind to Each Other

When Joel brings a jar full of caterpillars to a concert, one of them escapes! Will Ricky be able to keep his little brother out of trouble?

Proverbs 17:17 says, "A friend loves you all the time. A brother is always there to help you." Joel and Ricky's mom makes them go to the concert with Old Mr. Jones. As you read the story, can you think of a time when you were in a situation like Ricky and Joel?

"Ricky," Mom said one Saturday morning. "Remember what today is."

Mom and Ricky and Joel sat at the table. They were finished with breakfast.

"It is Saturday," Ricky said. "There is no school today. I can fly my kite. I can play street hockey. I can have fun."

"No," Mom said. "Remember? This afternoon, you are going to a concert with Joel and with Old Mr. Jones. He bought you the tickets. Remember?"

"Please," Ricky said. "Can Joel go alone with

Mr. Jones? I do not like concerts."

"Joel cannot go alone with Mr. Jones," Mom answered. "You are thirteen. Joel is seven. You have to look after him. Make sure nothing goes wrong."

"Please," Joel said. "Can Ricky go alone with Mr. Jones? I do not like concerts."

"Ricky cannot go alone with Mr. Jones," Mom said. "Remember, Mr. Jones is an old man who lives all alone. He needs friends. He is our neighbor, and I want both of you to keep him company."

"Yes, Mom," Ricky said.

"Yes, Mom," Joel said.

"Remember," Mom told Ricky. "Joel is only seven. You have to look after him. Make sure nothing goes wrong at the concert."

# 2

In the afternoon, there was a knock on the door.

Joel opened the door. It was Old Mr. Jones.

Old Mr. Jones wore a suit. He had gray hair. He had a big, big mustache.

"Hello, Mr. Jones," Joel said.

"Hello, Joel. Are you ready?"

"Yes," Joel said. He wore nice pants and a jacket. Ricky did, too. They were ready for the concert.

Mom and Ricky walked with Joel and Old Mr. Jones to the street.

Old Mr. Jones had a big, old car to drive them to the concert.

"Good-bye," Mom said to Joel.

"Good-bye," Mom said to Ricky.

"Good-bye," they said.

Ricky and Joel got into the backseat of the car.

Mom knocked on the window of the car before Old Mr. Jones drove away to the concert.

Ricky rolled the window down. "Yes?" he asked Mom.

"Remember," Mom told Ricky. "Joel is only seven. You have to look after him. Make sure nothing goes wrong at the concert."

# 3

"We will sit here," Old Mr. Jones said to Ricky and Joel.

Old Mr. Jones pointed to a place to sit. There were many people at the concert. Many people were already sitting down.

"Joel, I want you to sit on one side of me," Old Mr. Jones said.

"Ricky, I want you to sit on the other side of me," Old Mr. Jones said.

"Mr. Jones," Ricky said. "I think I should sit beside Joel. He is only seven. I have to look after him. I would not want anything to go wrong."

"What could go wrong?" Old Mr. Jones said. "He will be right beside me as we listen to the nice music."

"Yes, Mr. Jones," Ricky said.

They sat down. Ricky sat on one side of Mr. Jones. Joel sat on the other side of Mr. Jones. Old Mr. Jones and Ricky and Joel waited for the music to begin. Ricky remembered what Mom had told him. Ricky hoped nothing would go wrong.

But it did.

# 4

Soon after the music started, Old Mr. Jones fell asleep. It was nice music, but Old Mr. Jones needed a nap. He began to snore. No one could hear him snore because the music was louder than his snoring.

Ricky thought the music was nice, too. But he was afraid something might go wrong. He knew he should watch Joel.

Joel liked the music, too. But only for a little while. Then he wanted to play.

So Joel reached under his jacket. He had a glass jar under his jacket. It was a glass jar filled

with grass and caterpillars. He had brought the caterpillars from home.

Ricky looked across Old Mr. Jones to watch Joel. He saw Joel with the caterpillar jar.

"Joel," Ricky whispered. He was afraid to wake up Old Mr. Jones. "Please leave that jar alone. You should not have caterpillars at a concert."

The music was too loud. Joel did not hear what Ricky said. Joel shook the jar to make the caterpillars move. Joel tapped the jar to make the caterpillars move.

"Joel," Ricky said again. "Please leave that jar alone. You should not have caterpillars at a concert."

The music was too loud. Joel did not hear what Ricky said. Joel took the lid off of the glass jar of caterpillars.

# 5

Ricky wanted to take the glass jar of caterpillars from Joel. But he could not. Joel was sitting on the other side of Old Mr. Jones.

The music still played.

Old Mr. Jones still snored.

Ricky was still afraid to wake up Old Mr. Jones.

Joel still shook the glass jar of caterpillars. Only now the lid was off the glass jar. All of the grass and the caterpillars fell out.

There were ten caterpillars.

They fell into Joel's lap.

Ricky wanted to help Joel pick up the caterpillars. But he could not. Joel was sitting on the other side of Old Mr. Jones.

The music still played.

Old Mr. Jones still snored.

Ricky was still afraid to wake up Old Mr. Jones.

Joel looked for all ten of his caterpillars.

He found only nine caterpillars.

He looked and looked and looked.

Where was the other caterpillar?

# 6

Where was the other caterpillar? Joel looked on the floor. Joel looked beside him. Joel looked under him to see if he had sat on the other caterpillar.

The music still played.

Old Mr. Jones still snored.

Ricky was still afraid to wake up Old Mr. Jones.

And Joel still looked for the other caterpillar.

After a while, he stopped looking.

The music still played.

Old Mr. Jones still snored.

Ricky was still afraid to wake up Old Mr. Jones.

Then Joel saw the other caterpillar.

Then Ricky saw the other caterpillar.

The other caterpillar had crawled up the arm of Old Mr. Jones. Now it was on the neck of Old Mr. Jones.

The music still played.

Old Mr. Jones still snored.

Ricky was still afraid to wake up Old Mr. Jones.

And the other caterpillar crawled closer and closer to the big, bushy mustache of Old Mr. Jones.

# 7

Ricky remembered what Mom had said. Mom had told him to watch Joel. Mom had told him to make sure nothing went wrong.

Now there was a caterpillar crawling on the face of Old Mr. Jones.

The music still played.

Old Mr. Jones still snored.

Ricky was still afraid to wake up Old Mr. Jones.

Ricky had an idea.

He would roll up the paper of the program. He would roll up the paper into a tube. He

would reach up and knock that caterpillar off the face of Old Mr. Jones.

Ricky rolled up the paper of the program into a tube.

The music still played.

Old Mr. Jones still snored.

The caterpillar crawled onto the big, bushy mustache of Old Mr. Jones.

The music still played.

Old Mr. Jones still snored.

Ricky reached up to knock the caterpillar off of the big, bushy mustache with his tube of rolled-up paper.

Then something else went wrong.

The caterpillar was on the big, bushy mustache of Old Mr. Jones. It tickled his nose hairs.

The music still played.

But Old Mr. Jones finally woke up when the caterpillar tickled his nose hairs.

Old Mr. Jones suddenly lifted his head, just as Ricky tried to knock the caterpillar off the big, bushy mustache.

Instead of knocking away the caterpillar, Ricky hit Old Mr. Jones in the face with his rolled-up paper.

Old Mr. Jones tried to yell.

But something fell in his mouth.

Old Mr. Jones was so surprised, he snapped his mouth shut. His teeth snapped hard on the caterpillar.

Ricky looked at Old Mr. Jones.

Old Mr. Jones looked at Ricky.

Ricky tried to say something, but the music was too loud.

Old Mr. Jones tried to say something, but there was something in his mouth.

Old Mr. Jones did not know what was in his mouth.

He swallowed.

Then he looked down in his lap.

There it was.

The other half of the caterpillar. Still wriggling, with green stuff coming out.

# 9

Old Mr. Jones stood up.

The music still played.

"Come on," he said to Ricky. "We have to go."

"Come on," he said to Joel. "We have to go right away."

They left the concert. Joel took his glass jar of caterpillars with him. Although there were only nine caterpillars left.

Joel and Ricky and Old Mr. Jones went very quickly to the big, old car.

"Are you mad at me?" Ricky asked Old Mr. Jones when they got into the big, old car. "Mom told me to watch Joel so that nothing would go wrong. But it did. I am sorry."

"Are you mad at me?" Joel asked. "Is that why you are taking us home?"

"No, I am not mad," Old Mr. Jones said. "I have a funny taste in my mouth. The best way to get rid of the taste is to have some ice cream."

"Ice cream?" Ricky asked.

"Ice cream?" Joel asked.

"Ice cream," Old Mr. Jones said. "That is much more fun than a concert. Even if the music was nice."

"Yes, ice cream is much more fun," Ricky said.

"Yes, ice cream is much more fun," Joel said.

"There is only one thing," Old Mr. Jones said.

"Yes?" Ricky asked.

"Yes?" Joel asked.

"No more caterpillars!" Old Mr. Jones said.

So they went for ice cream.

And that is how Ricky and Joel became friends with Old Mr. Jones.

# A Lesson About Friendship

In *Bad Bug Blues*, Ricky and Joel don't want to go to the concert. When Joel's caterpillars get out of the jar, the boys are sure Mr. Jones will be mad at them.

Sometimes friendship comes in the places we least expect it. We can be kind to others, like Ricky and Joel were to Mr. Jones. Friendships often start by simply being kind to someone else.

# To Talk About

1. How should we treat our friends?

2. Who do you know that needs your kindness?

3. What can you do to show God's love to others?

*"May the Lord now be kind and true to you.*
*I will also be kind to you."*
*2 Samuel 2:6a*

Award-winning author Sigmund Brouwer inspires kids to love reading. From WATCH OUT FOR JOEL! to the ACCIDENTAL DETECTIVES series (full of stories about Joel's older brother, Ricky), Sigmund writes books that kids want to read again and again. Not only does he write cool books, Sigmund also holds writing camps and classes for more than ten thousand children each year!

You can read more about Sigmund, his books, and the Young Writer's Institute on his Web site, *www.coolreading.com*.